NOTHING

TO DO

DOUGLAS WOOD

illustrated by WENDY ANDERSON HALPERIN

DUTTON CHILDREN'S BOOKS

To Kathy, Bryan, and Eric,

my favorite people to do nothing with

—D W

To Schwibble, Mousey, Half Mast,

Lefty, Slick, Voots, Possum, Hoz, Kook, Fuzzy, and Chicken

—W A H

DUTTON CHILDREN'S BOOKS

A DIVISION OF PENGUIN YOUNG READERS GROUP

PUBLISHED BY THE PENGUIN GROUP

Penguin Group (USA) Inc., 375 Hudson Street, New York, New York 10014, U.S.A. •

Penguin Group (Canada), 90 Eglinton Avenue East, Suite 700, Toronto, Ontario, Canada

M4P 2Y3 (a division of Pearson Penguin Canada Inc.) • Penguin Books Ltd, 80 Strand,

London WC2R 0RL, England • Penguin Ireland, 25 St Stephen's Green, Dublin 2, Ireland

(a division of Penguin Books Ltd) • Penguin Group (Australia), 250 Camberwell Road,

Camberwell, Victoria 3124, Australia (a division of Pearson Australia Group Pty Ltd) •

Penguin Books India Pvt Ltd, 11 Community Centre, Panchsheel Park, New Delhi—110 017,

India • Penguin Group (NZ), Cnr Airborne and Rosedale Roads, Albany, Auckland 1310,

New Zealand (a division of Pearson New Zealand Ltd) • Penguin Books (South Africa)

(Pty) Ltd, 24 Sturdee Avenue, Rosebank, Johannesburg 2196, South Africa •

Penguin Books Ltd, Registered Offices: 80 Strand, London WC2R 0RL, England

Library of Congress Cataloging-in-Publication Data

Wood, Douglas, date.

Nothing to do / by Douglas Wood; illustrations by Wendy Anderson Halperin.

p. cm. Summary: Celebrates many ways of enjoying a day when the calendar is blank—

no homework, no soccer practice, no anything—from building a fort to lying down

and watching the clouds change shape. ISBN 0-525-47656-3 (alk. paper)

[1. Play—Fiction. 2. Recreation—Fiction.] I. Halperin, Wendy Anderson, ill. II. Title.

PZ7.W84738Not 2006 [E]–dc22 2005026246

Published in the United States by Dutton Children's Books,

a division of Penguin Young Readers Group

345 Hudson Street, New York, New York 10014

www.penguin.com/youngreaders

DESIGNED BY HEATHER WOOD WITH WENDY ANDERSON HALPERIN

Manufactured in China / First Edition

3 5 7 9 10 8 6 4 2

Artist's Note

I responded immediately when I received Douglas Wood's manuscript. I had recently seen a film by Richard Feather Anderson, which mentioned that in nature there are eight patterns in the way things grow. He had been inspired by a book called *Patterns in Nature*, by Peter S. Stevens, a teacher at MIT.

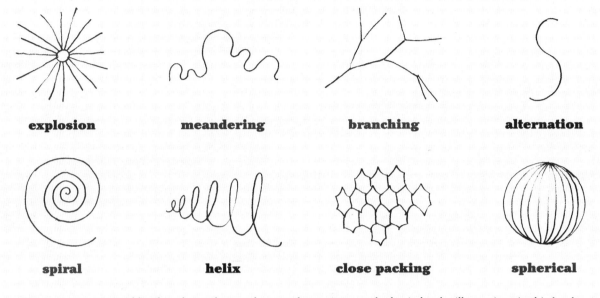

explosion   **meandering**   **branching**   **alternation**

spiral   **helix**   **close packing**   **spherical**

I, in turn, was inspired by this idea and wanted to use the patterns as the basis for the illustrations in this book. Sometimes I get an idea, but then my thoughts *meander* as I work it out; sometimes I do things over and over (like the *helix*). Sometimes I begin my work going in one direction, but I am influenced by something and I go off in a slightly different direction (like *branching*). *Alternation* is powerful in our lives—it is the push and pull of ideas. The splash of a rock hitting the water is a kind of *explosion*. Explosion is like a burst of inspiration. And I've started to notice the *spiral* everywhere in nature: it's in the fossil I find on the beach where I live, and in the sunflower in my garden.

When *Nothing to Do* came in my mailbox, I thought, we grow when we have nothing to do. Growth was the genesis of my illustrations.

Author's Note

This is a book I've wanted to write for a long time. I just didn't know it. In remembering my own childhood, I find that many of the happiest memories are not of special, planned activities or scheduled events, but of time I had to myself, to be myself. To daydream, to explore, to think up things to do with friends or on my own, and sometimes just to be bored and let life go along at its own unhurried speed.

Today the world moves at a faster pace, but kids still need unscheduled time—to relax, to imagine, to figure out who they are and how the world works. Kids still need time to do nothing. And so do people with big shoes.

P.S. There is a reason, after all, that we're called human *beings* and not human *doings*.

Once in a while, along comes a day when there is nothing—

absolutely, positively *nothing* . . . . .

. . . . to do.

And isn't that **great?**

No school. **No homework.** No Little League.
No dance class. **No play rehearsal.**
No soccer practice. No computer camp. . . .

No
anything!

Just a white, empty space on the calendar.

(Of course, some people get a little worried about these spaces. These people are very nice and wear big shoes. But we'll think about them a little later.)

But what do you do
    when there's *nothing to do?*

Well, I have heard stories, wonderful stories, about taking off your shoes and walking through green grass or mud—

in your bare feet!

Or making
toy ships out of
sticks and sailing them
across a puddle that
somehow seems as wide
as an ocean.

I've
heard about
lying on your back and
watching clouds turn from dinosaurs
into crocodiles into dragons into bears into butterflies
into . . . clouds.

Or lying on your stomach watching an ant
carry something three times bigger than he is
while you wonder, how can he do that?

And what do ants eat for breakfast
that makes them so strong?

I've heard of making a paper airplane
do loop-de-loops and barrel
rolls in the soft summer
air, then land smooth
as butter on
bread.

Or building a fort,
a secret place where no one can see you
because you can't see them. And surviving for hours
on peanut-butter sandwiches and lemonade.

I've heard about catching fireflies on a warm evening and putting them in a jar until you have two hands full of gold, and then letting them all go.

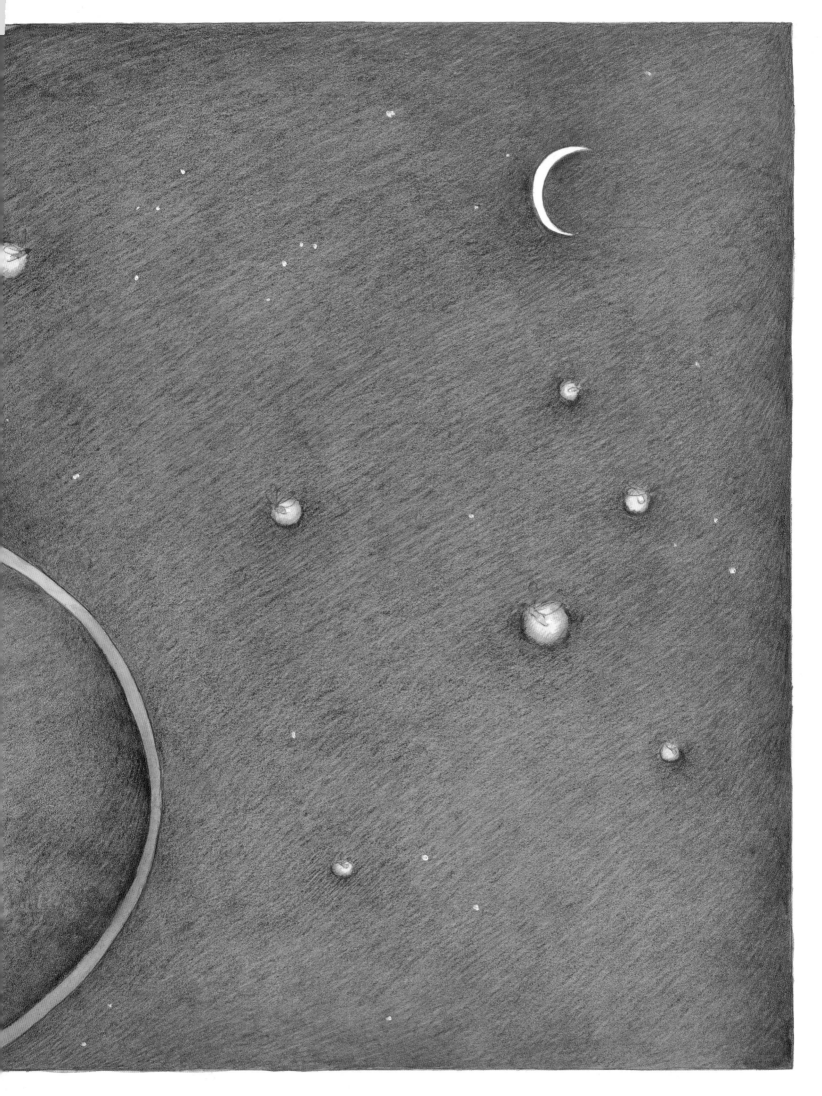

I've heard of swinging until
your toes touch the clouds. . . .
Or hanging by your knees like
a monkey, just to find out how
monkeys feel.

I've heard of climbing
a good tree that's been
waiting all its long life
just to be climbed by you.

Or finding a quiet spot and
reading your very favorite book.

And then reading it again . . .

. . . just because it *is* your favorite.

I've heard stories about exploring places

that really need to be explored. . . .

About making angels in
the snow, or igloos
or caves,

or sledding,
or tasting icicles,
or throwing snowballs,

or building round, fat men
with orange noses and old hats
who smile at everyone.

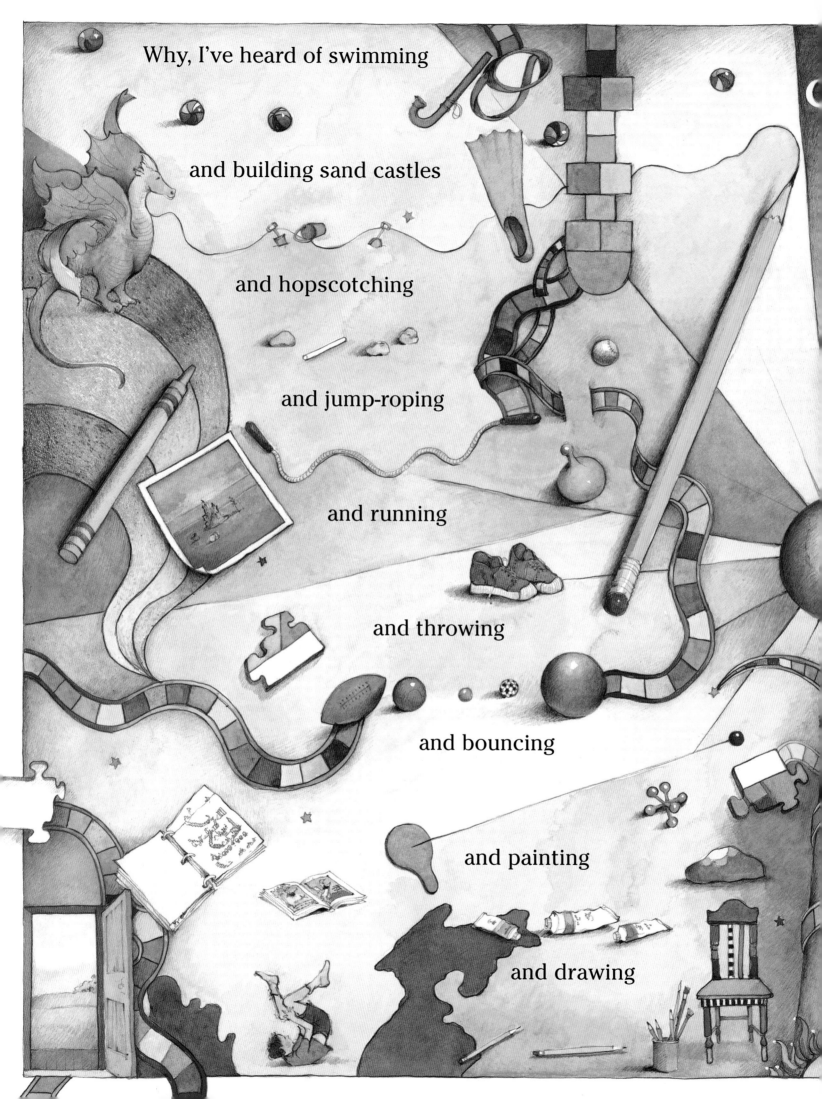

Why, I've heard of swimming

and building sand castles

and hopscotching

and jump-roping

and running

and throwing

and bouncing

and painting

and drawing

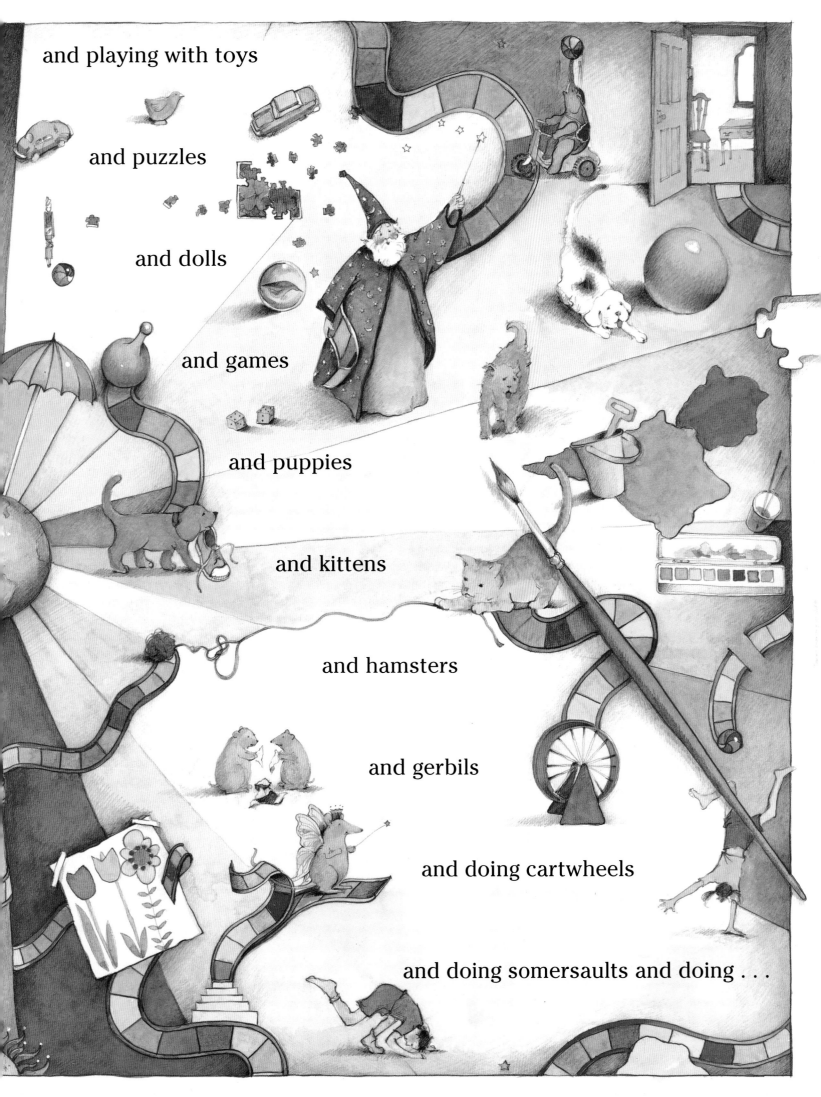

and playing with toys

and puzzles

and dolls

and games

and puppies

and kittens

and hamsters

and gerbils

and doing cartwheels

and doing somersaults and doing . . .

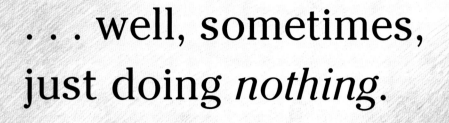

. . . well, sometimes,
just doing *nothing*.

And maybe one of
the *best* ways to do nothing
is to show someone else
how to do it.

Maybe even someone
with big shoes.

Just to remind them that, sometimes,
doing nothing is the most important thing
in the whole wide world to do.